Ronald
THE TOUGH SHEEP

Martin Waddell

Illustrated by
Chris Mould

OXFORD
UNIVERSITY PRESS

OXFORD
UNIVERSITY PRESS

Great Clarendon Street, Oxford OX2 6DP

Oxford University Press is a department of the University of Oxford.
It furthers the University's objective of excellence in research, scholarship,
and education by publishing worldwide in

Oxford New York

Auckland Bangkok Buenos Aires Cape Town Chennai
Dar es Salaam Delhi Hong Kong Istanbul Karachi Kolkata
Kuala Lumpur Madrid Melbourne Mexico City Mumbai Nairobi
São Paulo Shanghai Singapore Taipei Tokyo Toronto

with an associated company in Berlin

British Library Cataloguing in Publication Data

Data available

ISBN 0 19 919497 1

3 5 7 9 10 8 6 4 2

Guided Reading Pack (6 of the same title): ISBN 0 19 915576 5
Mixed Pack (1 of 6 different titles): ISBN 0 19 919499 8
Class Pack (6 copies of 6 titles): ISBN 0 19 919500 5

Printed in Hong Kong

Contents

Chapter 1

Ronald and the Goats

Ronald was a little lamb, but he wasn't white as snow.

His fleece was always a bit mucky. That was because he didn't skip about the field looking lovely like the other little lambs. He was a lamb who was different.

He tried to climb trees and jump puddles and he often fell in the mud.

"Don't just skip around!" Ronald told the other lambs. "Come with me and we'll have adventures!"

The little lambs huddled close to their mothers.

They wouldn't play with Ronald.

All they wanted to do was eat grass and look pretty, as little lambs do.

"OK!" Ronald said. "I'll go off and chase goats!"

"You can't do that, Ronald!" the little lambs baa-ed. "That's not what lambs do."

"Just watch me! I'm different!" said Ronald. "I can take on any goat in this field."

He ran at the goats going, "BAA-BAA-BAA-BAA." His legs were small, so he didn't catch any goats ... but he had great fun trying.

The goats weren't scared of Ronald, because he was still very little, but they didn't like being chased about by a lamb.

"Do something!" they complained to Chief Sheep, who was in charge of all the sheep in the field.

"Baa," said the Chief Sheep, but she sat still and did nothing.

She was thinking deep-sheep thoughts about green grass and sun.

"If you don't do something, we will!" muttered the goats. "If that lamb comes near us again, we'll mint-sauce him!"

It was the same with the old sheep dog, Rover. Rover came into the field to herd sheep, but he was herded himself.

Rover ended up in the sheep-pen, with Ronald standing outside, going, "BAA-BAA-BAA-BAA!"

Ronald was pretending to be a sheep dog.

Rover was fed up with Ronald.

"Get that little lamb off my tail!" he told Chief Sheep.

"Baa," the Chief Sheep agreed, but she still sat and did nothing. The Chief Sheep liked thinking, not doing.

"What can I do next?" Ronald asked the lambs.

"I know," said one lamb.
"The Chief Sheep is out there on the field. Why don't you take a run and jump over her?"

"Oh-er," said Ronald. Jumping over the Chief Sheep was something he had not thought of before.

"Go on, Ronald! We dare you!" the other lambs said.

"Watch me!" said Ronald.

Ronald wandered slowly down the field. Then he turned round and ran as fast as he could on his little lamb legs and ...

"Wheeeee … baaaaaaa!" Ronald jumped over the Chief Sheep.

"Baa!" said the Chief Sheep. She'd never been jumped over before, and she couldn't believe it had happened.

"Again, Ronald!" called all the lambs.
"We dare you to do it again."

"Whee-baa" and "whee-baa" and
"whee-baaa." Ronald did
it again

and again

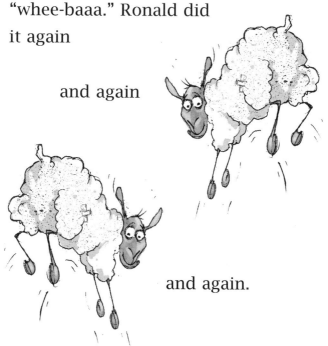

and again.

"BAAA!" went the Chief Sheep.

She stood up slowly, flicking her tail.
She had come to the end of her tether.
The Chief Sheep had never been
jumped over by a lamb before, and
she didn't like it one bit.

"I'll fix Ronald for good!" vowed the Chief Sheep.

She found Ronald down by the sheep-pen.

"Listen, young Ronald," she said. "Do you want to grow up to be a big sheep like me?"

Ronald looked at the Chief Sheep. She was fat and woolly, and spent all day going "Baa! Baa!" and bossing the others.

"I don't think I *do* want to grow up like you," Ronald said, being truthful. "I want to be a tough sheep."

"Go on that way and you won't grow up to be a big sheep at all!" the Chief Sheep said, angrily.

"Lambs aren't tough. Lambs are supposed to be skippy and cuddly."

"Well ... I'll try being cuddly," said Ronald.

But he soon found out that being cuddly wasn't much fun so ... Ronald went goat-chasing again.

He didn't mean to upset the goats. He just wanted to play.

"Don't *do* that!" they told Ronald.

"I'll give you a start," Ronald said. "Last goat to the end of the field is a nanny."

"Maa-maa!" went the goats getting cross.

"Maa-baaa!" went Ronald. And he maa-baaed them right round the field.

"That's IT!" decided the goats. "We've had enough of this game."

They all charged at Ronald and …

They won horns-down.

They butted and biffed and banged at poor Ronald and they chased him out of the field into Wolf Wood.

"Good riddance to bad rubbish!" the goats shouted. "We hope the Big Bad Wolf gets you! He'll eat you for sure."

Chapter 2

Ronald and the Big Bad Wolf

Ronald was brave, but he was a *little* lamb. He wasn't much more than a baby.

It was one thing to rush around the field going "baa-maa" at a few hairy old goats. It was quite another to take on the Big Bad Wolf.

Ronald was scared out of his little lamb-skin.

Along came a BIG BAD WOLF.

"Oh-baaaa!" Ronald thought.

The BIG BAD WOLF came up to Ronald, licking its lips.

"B-a-a-a-a-a!" Ronald wailed.

"What's your name, little lamb?" asked the wolf.

"I'm Ronald, the very brave lamb," Ronald quivered.

"Don't be scared of me, little lamb," said the wolf.

"Are you … are you the BIG BAD WOLF?" stammered Ronald.

"Well, I'm a wolf, and I'm big," said the wolf. "I don't know about bad. I suppose, as wolves go, I'm a bit of a softie."

"Are you going to eat me?" asked Ronald. He thought the wolf probably would. He'd been told about wolves by the Chief Sheep and Rover.

"Well ... no," said the wolf. "I'm a Mother Wolf. I have little ones of my own. I can see you are only a baby, so I am going to take care of you."

"Is that what wolves do?" Ronald gasped.

"It is what *this* wolf is doing," answered the wolf. "And what *this* wolf does, is what matters to you."

She picked Ronald up very gently, holding him by the scruff of his neck (which is what wolves do with their young) and carried him back to her den in the woods.

The wolf den was full of her cubs.

"Here comes Mum!" howled one.

"She's brought us a snack!" said another.

Ronald started to wriggle with fear, but he couldn't escape from the wolf's mouth. He thought the Big Bad Wolf had cheated him, and now he was going to be a wolf take-away supper.

The Mother Wolf laid him down on the ground. She put one paw on his back, so Ronald couldn't escape.

The wolf cubs gathered round the little lamb, licking their lips.

"Who are you?" they asked Ronald.

"I'm Ronald, the very b… b… b… brave lamb," stammered Ronald.

"Is Ronald our dinner?" the wolf cubs asked their mother.

"No," said the Mother Wolf.
"Ronald's only a baby. I'm going to look after him, just like I look after you."

"Is that what wolves do?" the smallest wolf cub asked her mother.

"It is what *this* wolf is doing," answered the Mother Wolf. "And what *this* wolf does, is what matters to you."

Chapter 3

Ronald in the Wolves' Den

Ronald stayed with Mother Wolf and her cubs.

He made special friends with the smallest wolf cub.

The smallest wolf cub liked having someone in the den who was smaller than she was. She got bounced on a lot by her big sisters and brothers.

"I like playing with you, because you're not rough and tough like the others," she told Ronald.

"I *am* rough and tough for a lamb," Ronald said, feeling hurt.

"Rough and tough for a lamb doesn't count much when you're playing with wolves!" the smallest wolf cub told him.

Ronald learned all the wolf games, playing with her. He grew into a very big sheep.

The smallest wolf cub grew into a wolf, but she still wasn't as big as the others.

The young wolves ran like the wind, but Ronald couldn't keep up because his legs were too little.

The wolves howled at the moon and the stars, to scare all the sheep in the fields around the edge of the wood.

Ronald tried to howl too, but his "baa" didn't sound right. Some of the wolves laughed at Ronald. They didn't think he was much of a wolf.

"You go 'baa-yeoooo' when we howl at the moon," they told Ronald. "'Baa-yeoooo' sounds silly to us."

"Ronald's doing his best," the smallest wolf told the others.

But Ronald was very upset. He went and sat by himself, feeling sulky.

The kind Mother Wolf saw this, and she called Ronald to her.

"You're too gentle to live in the wood," she told Ronald. "One of these days some wolf might eat you, by mistake. You'd better go back where you belong, with the sheep."

Ronald was sad when Mother Wolf led him to the edge of Wolf Wood, and made him go back to the fields. She was a kind wolf, and it seemed to her to be the best thing to do.

The smallest wolf was sad, too.

"I'll miss Ronald!" she said to her mother. "I like him, because he isn't as big and rough as my sisters and brothers."

"That's because Ronald's a sheep," said her mother.

"He should be with other sheep. They don't howl at the moon and they won't mind if he baas. That is what sheep do."

"Ronald is different," said the smallest wolf.

But that didn't bring Ronald back.

Chapter 4

Ronald and the Big Bad Farmer

Ronald trotted into a field. It wasn't the one that he'd lived in when he was a lamb.

Along came a farmer and at the end of the field, he saw a lost sheep.

It was Ronald ... and Ronald was scared.

Ronald had heard all about farmers from the wolves in the den.

"It's the Big bad Farmer," he cried and he tried to run away. But even a sheep who has been running with wolves isn't that fast, because of the short-leg problem.

"Got you!" cried the farmer.

Ronald kicked and struggled and baa-ed, but he couldn't escape.

"The Big Bad Farmer has got me!" thought Ronald, and he shivered and shook.

"Don't be scared of me, sheep!" said the farmer. "I'll look after you."

The farmer thought Ronald had strayed from his flock and that was why he was scared.

The farmer took Ronald back to his flock.

"In you go," said the farmer, and he put Ronald into a field full of sheep.

"I'm not afraid of strange sheep!" Ronald decided, and he ran toward the others. "Hello, I'm Ronald, the brave sheep," he said.

What the others saw looked like a sheep, but it loped like a WOLF …

Chapter 5

Ronald and the Strange Sheep

The sheep gathered around Ronald, and they sniffed the air.

They smelled W-O-L-F.

"Baa ... baaa ... baaa," went the sheep, and they backed away.

"Baa-yeooo!" went Ronald, answering back.

That didn't help.

"You don't baa like us. You're not a sheep, you're a wolf!" said the sheep.

"I'm not a wolf," Ronald replied.

"Do 'baa' again!" said the sheep.

"Baa-yeooo!" went Ronald.

"Wolf … definitely!" said the others.

"Sheep," Ronald insisted. "A sheep who is just a bit different!"

"We've never heard of a sheep who went 'yeooo!'" said the others.

Then the Wisest Ram came out of the flock.

He took a close look at Ronald, but he kept a safe distance away.

"Baa-yeooo! I'm a sheep!" Ronald said, hopefully.

"You smell like a wolf," the Wisest Ram said. "And you howl like a wolf."

"Who ever heard of a wolf who went 'baa'?" Ronald said. He went "baa" again just to show them, but of course his "baa" came out "baa-yeooo!"

The Wisest Ram put his head on one side, and considered. Then he drew back to the far end of the field, and he had a Sheep-Talk with the rest.

"We'll take a vote!" they decided.

The result of the vote was: fourteen tails to four against Ronald being a sheep.

The Wisest Ram came back to Ronald.

"Go away!" he told Ronald.

"Why?" Ronald said.

"You're a wolf dressed up like a sheep," the Wisest Ram said.

"No, I'm not!" Ronald said, and he went 'baa-yeoo' in distress.

"That proves you are a wolf!" cried the ram.

The sheep all moved away down the field with the Wisest Ram, "baaing" amongst themselves.

"Beware of the wolf who calls himself Ronald," they said, and they told all their lambs to stay out of his way.

Chapter 6

Ronald the Fierce

Poor Ronald was left all alone at one end of the field.

The sheep wouldn't go near him.

The goats were just the same.

The sheep dog left him out when she was herding the others. Sheep dogs are never happy with wolves.

Ronald's end of the field was the end that was nearest Wolf Wood and Ronald was missing his friends, especially the smallest wolf.

Night fell and he went "baa-yeoo" at the moon when it rose. The other sheep huddled down at their end of the field. They stayed close together and listened, and shivered and shook.

But one night, things changed.

The sheep lay in the field in the moonlight.

The farmer lay in bed in his house.

The old sheep dog lay by the fire, fast asleep.

Then, down the farm lane, soft footed and hunting together, came a pair of small yappy dogs.

Their names were Trixie and Dixie and they'd come down from town for the weekend. Their owners had brought rubber bones they could chew, and small toys that squeaked for the two dogs to chase.

"Toys are dumbo stuff!" Trixie told Dixie. "Look in that field. I see SHEEP!"

"What are sheep for?" Dixie asked Trixie.

"Sheep are for biting!" said Trixie.

They slipped through the hedge, and ran into the field, barking like mad at the sheep.

The sheep ran round the field on their little sheep legs, but they couldn't escape from the nipping and biting and barking.

All but one sheep.

One brave sheep stood still, as the dogs ran at him.

It was Ronald, of course.

He was used to wolves, so two yappy dogs didn't scare him at all.

The wool bristled on Ronald's back.

"BAA-YEOOOOO!" Ronald howled, and he stopped the two dogs in their tracks.

"What's that?" gasped Dixie.

"I don't know," said Trixie. "But I know I don't like it!"

And then …

… Ronald charged straight at them, baring his little sheep teeth.

"Oh-er!" quaked Trixie. "I know what that is now! It's a wolf!"

And she ran away, because she couldn't tackle a wolf.

Dixie took one look, and he ran after Trixie, with Ronald "baa-yeooing" behind him.

They escaped through the hole in the hedge, though they took a few cuts from the briars and the brambles that scratched their soft noses.

"I'm not going back there again," Trixie told Dixie.

"No, never, ever!" said Dixie.

Ronald came back from the chase.

The other sheep gathered round at their end of the field, for another Sheep-Talk.

"Wolves don't save sheep!" one of them said. "Ronald can't be a wolf. He's a sheep."

"Sheep don't chase dogs!" said another. "So Ronald can't be a sheep, either."

"Whatever he is, we must thank him for saving our wool," they decided.

Then they all marched up the field to see Ronald. They came close to him … but not too close.

"HURRAH FOR RONALD, OUR SHEEP-WOLF!" they bleated.

"Who?" Ronald said.

"That's you," said the sheep. "You're our Sheep Wolf. You saved our wool from those dogs."

"Well … if that's what you think I am, you can call me a sheep-wolf," sighed Ronald, because he didn't mind being different.

"Now, they're going to be my friends," Ronald thought … but he was wrong!

Chapter 7

Ronald Finds Where He Belongs

Sheep are sheepy by nature.

They gave Ronald some good grass to eat and a medal made from an acorn, but they were still scared.

"We are sheep, and sheep have to be careful with wolves," they told Ronald, and they stayed away from his end of the field, just in case.

Ronald prowled at his end of the field, with no friends.

He howled at the moon, because he was so lonely. "BAA-YEOOO! BAA-YEOOO! BAA-YEOOO!"

And then, from far away, somewhere deep in the Wood, Ronald heard the cry of a wolf.

It was the smallest wolf, answering Ronald and calling him back to Wolf Wood.

Ronald's wool prickled up on his back. He ran round the field trying to find a way out.

"What are you doing?" cried all the sheep.

"I'm going back to Wolf Wood, where I belong!" Ronald said.

"Got you this time!" said the sheep. "Sheep don't go into Wolf Wood. We stay where we are, in the fields."

"Not this sheep!" said Ronald. "I'm different!"

And he wolf-leaped over the fence, running away towards Wolf Wood, and his friend the smallest wolf.

"Hello, Wolf!" Ronald said, when he met the smallest wolf.

"Hello, Sheep," the smallest wolf replied.

They nuzzled each other, the way that wolves do when they meet.

Ronald stayed with the smallest wolf. He trusted his friend.

"The other wolves will have to eat me first, if they want to eat you," the smallest wolf told Ronald. "Just let them try!"

They're still together, somewhere in
Wolf Wood.

You'll know them if one night you
hear a wolf pack howl at the moon
and one of them (not the loudest
by far) is going …

About the author

I met Ronald once. There was a field behind my house, and in the field were a lot of bored sheep ... and Ronald.

He came right up to the fence, instead of ignoring me, like the others. He looked at me, with a glint in his eye. Sheep don't do that.